Chanukah is coming
Danny Draydl is feeling blue
He doesn't know how to spin
And he doesn't know what to do

DANNY the DIZZY DRAYDL

**words and pictures
by Cheryl Gunsher**

published by

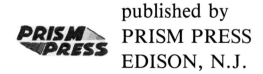

PRISM PRESS
EDISON, N.J.

0 9 8 7 6 5 4 3 2 1

Dedicated to the memory of
Kate Schmukler Frieman z″l

It was the Hebrew month of Kislev, and all the draydls were preparing for their favorite holiday.

All year long the special tops, called draydls, lay in boxes,
and leaned alone on shelves.

But Chanukah was coming soon, and children
were finding their draydls to practice spinning them.

The children were excited thinking about Chanukah, a favorite time of the year when they have so much fun.

Everyone was eagerly awaiting the 8 days of singing and dancing and playing with their draydls. Almost everyone, at least . . .

You see, there was one draydl, named
Danny, who wasn't looking forward to
this special holiday because he had a problem
every Chanukah. Unlike all of the other draydls who loved
to spin and spin during Chanukah, Danny Draydl became
dizzy every time someone spinned him!

Danny didn't know what to do. He wanted to be spun and to dance like the other draydls, (after all, that is what draydls are supposed to do). But every time Danny was spun, he got so dizzy he fell down.

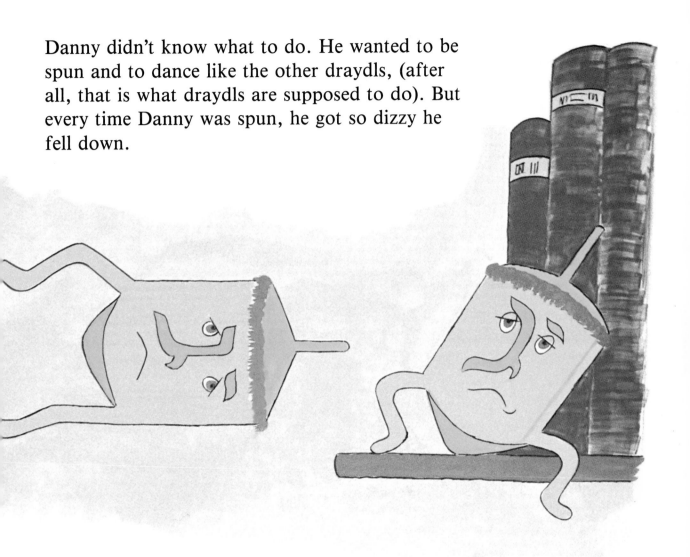

It wasn't much fun to play with Danny and
so the children left him on the shelf and
played with the other draydls. Of
course, this made Danny unhappy.
He didn't want to sit on the
shelf while the other draydls
were all having fun being
spun round and round
by the joyful children.

So, Danny went to visit the other draydls to see if they could teach him the secret of how to spin without becoming dizzy. First, he went to Sammy Draydl and asked him. Sammy told him to try and keep his eyes closed so that he wouldn't see everything spinning around him. Maybe that would help. Danny tried closing his eyes while he spun, but he bumped into everything and that made him even dizzier.

He then went to Debbie Draydl for advice. She told him to take deep breaths and that might help. So, Danny started taking deep breaths when he was spun, but he breathed so deeply that he fell over on his back and that hurt.

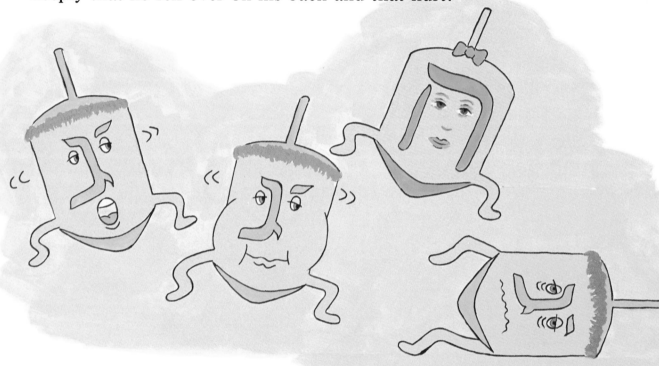

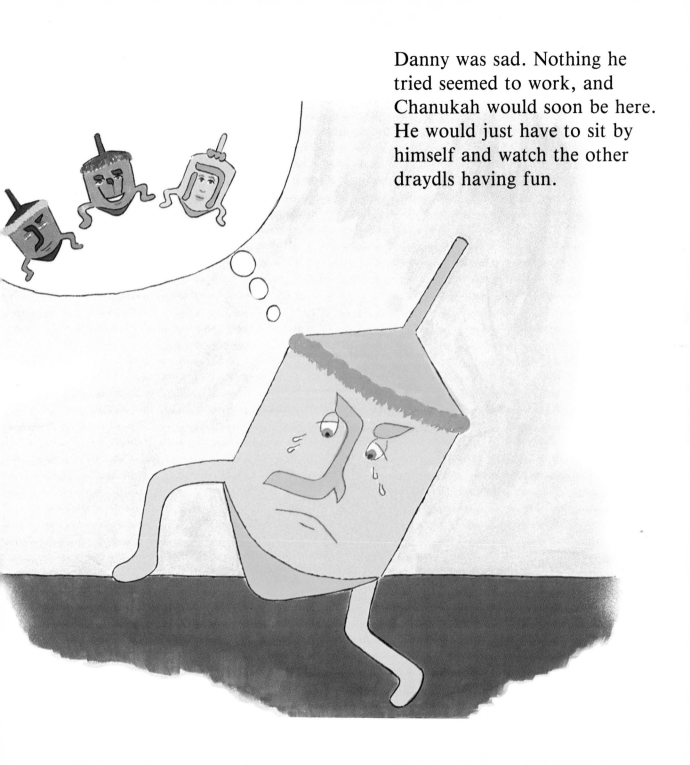

Danny was sad. Nothing he tried seemed to work, and Chanukah would soon be here. He would just have to sit by himself and watch the other draydls having fun.

Then, Ben Draydl, who had seen Danny sitting sadly by himself, said to him, "listen, the father who lives in my house has an old wooden draydl that he has had since he was a little boy. Maybe the wise old wooden draydl can help you with your problem." Danny said, "I hope so. Where can I find him?" "Father keeps him on a special shelf with the other special things like the shofar that he blows on Rosh Hashanah and the spice box that he uses at the end of Shabbat," explained Ben.

"Okay," said Danny. "Let's go find the wise old draydl and see if he can help me." So, they climbed up onto the shelves, higher and higher and higher until they reached the shelf where they found the shofar, the spice box, and the wise old wooden draydl.

"Here we are," said Danny. Then they walked over to the old wooden draydl and introduced themselves. "I'm Danny, and this is my friend Ben," Danny said. "I have a problem and I am hoping you can help me."

The old wooden draydl, whose name was Rabbi Judah, told
them that he had known other draydls who had had trouble
with spinning. He then told Danny what he should do.

"Draydls aren't just toys," said Rabbi Judah Draydl. "They have another purpose, too." "What is that?" asked Danny. "All draydls have four letters," said Rabbi Judah, "a נ (nun), a ג (gimel), an ה (heah), and a ש (shin)." "Do you know what these letters stand for?"

"No, please tell us," said Danny and Ben. "They stand for **nas gadol hayah sham**, which means a great miracle happened there," said Rabbi Judah. "Where?" asked Danny and Ben. "In the land of Israel," said Rabbi Judah. "The 4 letters you have on your sides stand for the miracle of Chanukah when the oil that was only to have kept the menorah lit for just one day burned for 8 days."

"When you are spinning," said Rabbi Judah, "children are not only playing a game, but are also celebrating the miracle of Chanukah, and that is an important mitzvah. From now on, every time you spin and dance, remember the important message for which your letters stand and you won't become dizzy anymore."

Danny suddenly felt very proud of being a draydl and he began to spin and spin and he didn't get dizzy, **not at all!**

The first night of Chanukah was the best one Danny could remember.
He danced and spun and had the best time he ever had. He was very
thankful for the wise old wooden draydl who had taught him the
miracle of Chanukah.